The King of Kites

Judith Heneghan
and Laure Fournier

READZONE

Anil knew about kites.

He knew how to make them out of paper, sticks and glue. He knew how to fly them in the sky above the village.

4

The other children brought him their
broken kites to mend.

Anil was the King of Kites.

Anil's mother knew how to sew.
     She knew how to cut cloth and stitch seams. She knew how to work beautiful patterns in bright silk.

The other women brought her their old clothes to mend.

She was the Queen of Needles.

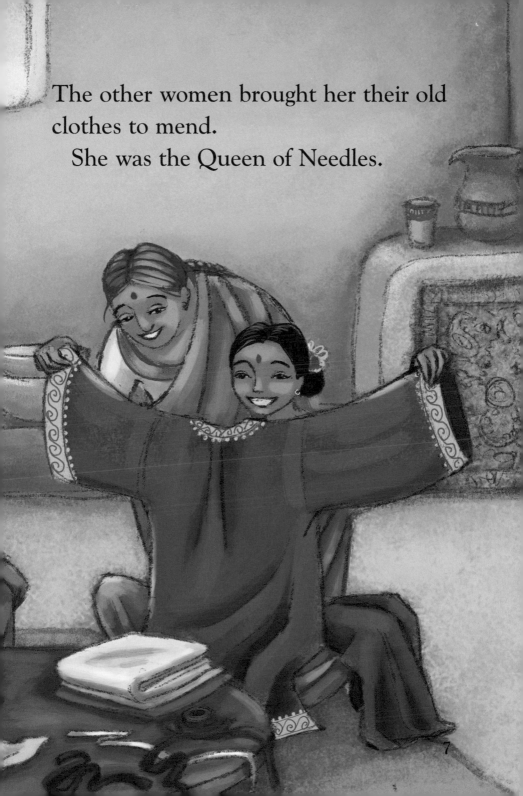

Every morning, Anil and his
mother sat down in a corner of
the yard.

Anil's mother had everything she needed: folds of fabric, reels of thread and a pot of shiny new pins.

She set to work and soon her needle flew.

Anil, too, had everything he needed:
sheets of paper, spools of string and a
pot of good strong glue. He set to work
and soon his fingers flew.

Then, one day, Anil heard about a wedding in the village.

"I shall make twelve kites and fly them all at once in honour of the bride," said Anil to his friends. "I shall cover them with sequins and give them tails of bright ribbon."

He sat down in the shade and set to work.

But Anil's mother was not pleased.

"I shall have extra shirts and saris to sew for the wedding!" she cried. "You don't have time for kites, Anil! I need your help, and I need your sequins and your ribbon!"

It was true. The whole village wanted
new clothes for the wedding.

16

Anil's mother sat down in the
shade and set to work.
All day long she cut and sewed
and stitched.

"I need more cloth!" she cried, and Anil ran straight to the market.

"I need more thread!" she cried, and back he went again.

"Anil!" called his friends. "Where are the twelve new kites for the wedding?"

Anil did not answer. His mother had cut up his kite paper for her sari patterns. She had used his string when she ran out of thread.

21

By nightfall all the new clothes were ready. But Anil felt sad. How could he go to the wedding without the kites?

Anil's friends saw that he was sad. They had not forgotten his promise to fly kites at the wedding.

When Anil woke up the next morning, twelve kites lay on the ground outside his house – the kites he had made for his friends long ago!

"Quick!" said his mother. "I saved
a few sequins! And one roll of ribbon!
Fetch my needle! Fetch the glue!"
Anil's mother helped him to
decorate the kites.

At the wedding, everyone praised Anil's mother for her stitching.

She was the Queen of Needles.

And everyone admired Anil's twelve beautiful kites flying high in the sky.

Anil thanked his friends for giving him their kites. They laughed and lifted him up onto their shoulders.

"You made them for us, Anil!" they shouted. "You are the King of Kites!"

Did you enjoy this book?

Look out for more *Swifts* titles –
stories in 500 words